LOCKED IN THE ZOO, WHAT WILL THEY DO?

by GLADYS DORFMAN

Illustrated by Roc Goudreau
Created and Designed by Gladys Dorfman

Published in the United States by
   Hannah Mae Enterprises, Inc.
   P.O. Box 81143
   Springfield, MA 01138-1143
Text copyright © 2000 by Gladys Dorfman
Illustrations copyright © 2000 by Gladys Dorfman

Printed in the United States by Arrow Printing. Bemidji, Minnesota.

   Publisher's Cataloging-in-Publication
   (Provided by Quality Books, Inc.)
Dorfman, Gladys
   Locked in the zoo, what will they do?
   by Gladys Dorfman. -- 1st ed.
   p. cm.
   LCCN: 00-26098
   ISBN: 0-9671111-2-9
   SUMMARY: Five children join grandma in a visit to the zoo.

   1. Zoos--Juvenile fiction. 2. Grandparent and child--Juvenile fiction.
   3. Stories in rhyme. I. Title.

PZ8.3.D6746Lo 2000   [E]
          QBI00-500087

This book is dedicated to the zoos around

the world, especially the Zoo In Forest Park

where the author spent many happy,

memorable hours as a child.

Tiffanie, Stephanie, Christopher, Matthew, and Jesse, too,

went with Grandma to the zoo.

2

It was half past eight as all six stood at the gate. The gate was locked. What will they do? They could not get inside the zoo.

3

4

Uphill,

5

downhill,
to the back of the zoo they went.

6

The gate was locked. What will they do?
How do they get inside the zoo?

Tiffanie, Stephanie, Christopher, Matthew, and Jesse, too, returned with Grandma to the front of the zoo. It was half past nine. They were on time. Everything was just fine.

8

At half past one, they were having fun.
They sat and ate inside the gate.

Hippopotamus

Cougar

At half past two, they were all still inside the zoo.

Fallow Deer

At half past three, they
did not want to leave.

At half past four, they
still wanted to see more.

Tiger

13

Lion

14

When it was late at half past eight,
they could not find the big front gate.

Zebra

Red Fox

15

Around and around to the back of the zoo they went. The gate was locked. What will they do? How do they get outside the zoo?

16

The zookeeper's checking
time was half past nine.

Polar
Bear

Uphill, downhill, to the back of the zoo he went.

Tiffanie, Stephanie, Christopher, Matthew, and Jesse, too, with Grandma followed the zookeeper to the front of the zoo.

Sheep

Elephant

At half past ten, everyone was safely home again.

22

Facts About the Animals Seen on the Opposite Page

Cougar

A native of North and South America. A large animal with a long, slender body is a member of the cat family.

Ring-Tail Lemur

A native of Madagascar, an island off the southeast coast of Africa. A monkey-like animal with large round eyes, a black and white-ringed furry tail and human-like hands.

Red Fox

A native of North America. A slender animal with pointed nose and ears, a bushy tail, and paws that resemble feet with little boots on them.

Black Bear

A native of North America. Much smaller than the Arctic polar bear. It has long, strong, curved paws for climbing trees, digging roots and logs, and finding honey-combs and grubs to eat. The bear eats all summer and fall to gain weight to prepare itself for the winter months of hibernation. Temperature and availability of food determines how long the bear hibernates. In milder climates, the bear may hibernate for less than six weeks or not at all.

Fallow Deer

A native of England and Europe. Some fallow deer are tan with white spots. Others are chocolate brown with lighter brown dots. Unlike the cow, whose horns are made of keratin (a substance similar to our fingernails), male fallow deer have antlers made of bone. They shed their antlers in April and begin to grow new ones. While the new antlers are growing, they are covered with soft velvet-like skin. After the antlers are fully grown, the deer rub against trees and stones to rub off the velvet-like skin. Female fallow deer do not grow antlers.

Match the names of the animals to the pictures.

Cougar

Red Fox

Black Bear

Fallow Deer

Ring-Tail Lemur

The author thanks her mother for taking her to the zoo. It was those happy childhood memories that inspired her to write this book.

Special thanks to Carol McCray Davies of the Forest Park Zoological Society for graciously providing information about many of the animals used in this book.